Town Mouse and Country Mouse

Retold by Laurel Dickey
Illustrated by Mayme Crouse

Pioneer Valley Educational Press, Inc.

Town Mouse went to see
Country Mouse.

"Come in, come in,"
said Country Mouse.
"Come in and see my house."

3

"Here is some food,"
said Country Mouse.

"Oh, I don't like your food,"
said Town Mouse.
"And I don't like your house.
Come to town and
see my house."

5

Country Mouse went to see
Town Mouse.
"Come in, come in,"
said Town Mouse.
"Come in and see my house."

"I like your house,"
said Country Mouse.

"Here is some food,"
said Town Mouse.

"Oh, I like your food,"
said Country Mouse.

Town Mouse and
Country Mouse
went out for a walk.
They saw a big cat.

"Oh, no! Run! Run!"
said Town Mouse.

Town Mouse and
Country Mouse ran and ran.

Town Mouse and
Country Mouse
saw a big dog.

"Oh, no! Run! Run!"
said Town Mouse.

Town Mouse and
Country Mouse ran and ran.

"I like your house, and
I like your food,
but I do **not**
like your town,"
said Country Mouse.
"I'm going home
and staying home!"